Books by Clara Vulliamy

MARSHMALLOW PIE THE CAT SUPERSTAR

MARSHMALLOW PIE THE CAT SUPERSTAR: ON TV

MARSHMALLOW PIE THE CAT SUPERSTAR: IN HOLLYWOOD

MARSHMALLOW PIE THE CAT SUPERSTAR: ON STAGE

*The Dotty Detective series
in reading order*

DOTTY DETECTIVE

THE PAW PRINT PUZZLE

THE MIDNIGHT MYSTERY

THE LOST PUPPY

THE BIRTHDAY SURPRISE

THE VACATION MYSTERY

Marshmallow Pie the Cat Superstar On Stage

Clara Vulliamy

HarperCollins *Children's Books*

First published in the United Kingdom by
HarperCollins *Children's Books* in 2021
Published in this edition in the USA by HarperCollins *Children's Books* in 2022
HarperCollins *Children's Books* is a division of HarperCollins*Publishers* Ltd
1 London Bridge Street
London SE1 9GF

www.harpercollins.co.uk

1

HarperCollins*Publishers*
1st Floor, Watermarque Building, Ringsend Road
Dublin 4, Ireland

ISBN 978-0-00-846137-9

Clara Vulliamy asserts the moral right to be identified as the author
and illustrator of the work.
A CIP catalog record for this title is available from the British Library.

Printed and bound in the UK using 100%
renewable electricity at CPI Group (UK) Ltd

This book is produced from independently certified FSC™ paper
to ensure responsible forest management.

For more information visit: www.harpercollins.co.uk/green

For Elorine, with much love

The Stage

The attic where junk and antiques are kept

MASS mirror me to myself

Elegant Sofa

I sit here in the BEST spot

Lady Everett's desk

Jewelry box

Dog bed

Tasty Crumbs

← Unattended vendor's tray

≡ Chapter One ≡
An Uninvited Guest

Oh, hello. My name is Marshmallow Pie
and I am a GLOBAL SUPERSTAR.

I recently starred in a Hollywood movie. My human, Amelia, took me to the premiere at a very fancy movie theater. When we arrived on the red carpet, my fans pressed forward to take my photograph, then we went inside to watch the film on an enormous screen.

Amelia and her friend Zack wrote
about it in their school newspaper, the
Fluffington Post.

Marshmallow Pie's
MOVIE PREMIERE

Loads of famous actors were there to
see the film, and hundreds of fans too!
Pie was FANTASTIC. All the reviews
were 5 STARS !!! ☆ ☆ ☆ ☆ ☆

HUGE screen ↓

Fancy snacks
for Pie →

Guinea
Pig Has
TRIPLETS!

Things are a little less glamorous behind the scenes. Today Amelia is sorting the laundry, and I am offering valuable help by sitting in the laundry basket, supervising. She gives me a friendly scratch under the chin.

I **STRETCH** luxuriously. Life is good. I have Amelia, and I'm a famous celebrity now, admired all over the world. What could possibly go wrong?

The doorbell rings.

It's our neighbor from the apartment below—Buster's human. Buster is an actor too, and my greatest rival. Whenever I get ahead in my sparkling career, that pesky dog seems to catch up with lucky break of his own.

I can hear our neighbor talking loudly to Amelia and her dad.

"Could you look after Buster for a few days?" she's saying.

Wait, *what?* No! NO WAY!

"He'll be no trouble," she carries on.

"I'm going on an important work trip—very short notice—and my usual extremely classy kennels are all booked up. . . . He's used to the finer things, but I suppose he'll be all right here, just this once."

And without waiting for an answer, she hands Amelia lots of heavy bags overflowing with Buster's belongings.

Then she promptly turns around and leaves—allowing that big, slobbering dog to burst into our home.

I am **APPALLED!**

Buster is wearing his black leather jacket, and he barks loudly as he charges around the apartment. Then he catches sight of me. He bounds up to the laundry basket and knocks it over, sending me tumbling out. I land under a pile of socks and dishtowels.

Amelia's dad chuckles and shakes his head. "I'm pretty busy with work at the moment, Amelia," he says, "so the dog-sitting duties will be mainly up to you!"

"I'll do my best. I love ALL different animals, and I've never looked after a dog before!" she answers happily. "As long as Pie doesn't mind. . . ."

Doesn't mind? Let me tell you, I am *furious.* I flatten my ears back and give a low hiss.

Hissss!

But nobody notices, because Buster is now tipping over the bags his human left and wildly pulling out his toys.

He pushes a rubber chicken into Amelia's hand. Then, just as quickly, he grabs it in his mouth and tries to snatch it back. *How rude!*

"Yay—tug of war!" Amelia says, laughing.

But all I see is a rough dog with NO social graces. I'm sure she's only playing with Buster to be polite.

As the day goes on, Buster follows me
EVERYWHERE. When I go out onto
the balcony for a snooze in the sunshine,
he comes to bother me. When I play
with my toys, he tries to take over.

WOOF!

And worst of all, when I curl up on the sofa with Amelia to watch TV, she pats the space next to her and Buster jumps up too! It's a SQUASH.

I wish he wasn't here . . . *especially* because I have a FRUITY onesie I like to wear for cozy evenings in, but I do NOT want to be seen in it by anyone outside the family. It's getting a little tight around the middle and the buttons keep bursting open.

Now it's bedtime. Buster has a **MASSIVE** bed shaped like a sports car that takes up most of the living room, so there's hardly any space left for me. Buster gets into his sports car and I settle down on my pillow.

"Goodnight, you two," says Amelia. "Be good!" And she goes to bed too.

I *didn't invite Buster for a sleepover*, I think to myself. He's getting far too much attention. There has to be something in it for me.

I won't show you how I managed it. All I will say is this . . .

When Amelia comes in the next morning, there has been a change in the sleeping arrangements.

Chapter Two
Cat Burglar

I am hiding from Buster in the broom closet. I can hear him snuffling about outside and whining because he can't find me.

But I can't avoid him forever, because Amelia is calling us for breakfast and I *never* miss a meal. Buster and I have to eat together, so I am obliged to budge over and make space for his **HUGE** bowl and massive portion of food. (Not fair, if you ask me.)

His table manners are **UNSPEAKABLE.**

The phone rings. It's Dexter, my agent from the Ace Animal Acting Agency, calling to speak to Amelia.

After she hangs up, she turns to me excitedly. "Pie, there's a fantastic new opportunity for you," she says, "at the Theater Royale—the best theater in town!"

Ah, some *good* news! Things are looking up. This could be my chance to become a celebrated stage actor!

"It's a play called *The Everett Emeralds*, about a cat burglar at a grand country house—" Amelia pauses. "What *is* a cat burglar, Dad?"

"It's a thief who breaks into high windows by climbing up buildings and over rooftops," he tells her. "Agile and light on their feet, like a cat."

THE EVERETT EMERALDS

Directed by Patricia Hastings
Coming soon to the Theater Royale!

Of course, I think to myself, landing heavily on a pillow. I find a Shrimp Crunchie behind the sofa cushions and eat it. We cats *are* delicate, dainty, and oh so graceful.

"Well, they are also looking for a *real* cat to star in the play," Amelia carries on, giving me a quick brush. "But we don't have much time to get ready. The audition is at the agency this afternoon!"

"I have a work meeting," Amelia's dad tells her. "You'll have to take Buster with you."

On hearing his name, Buster jumps to his feet eagerly.

I am SO annoyed. When Buster turned up at my first ever audition, things did *not* go well. I hope he stays in the background today and doesn't cramp my style.

When we arrive at the audition, Amelia says hello to Dexter.

"Take a seat, folks," he says to us. "The play's director, Patricia Hastings, will see you soon."

So we sit down to wait. Buster insists on sitting right in the middle.

"Just think," Amelia says excitedly, "this will be a live show in front of a REAL audience! We've never done anything like this before!"

I look around. There are lots of other cats auditioning too . . .

. . . but none are as *magnificent* as me. When at last it's my turn, I show off all my biggest, fanciest, and BEST moves.

My Best Moves

"Marvelous, marvelous!"

Patricia cries enthusiastically. "Marshmallow Pie will be perfect for the role." And she casts me then and there.

At that moment, I glimpse a familiar figure striding toward us, mopping his brow with a silk handkerchief. My nose tickles at the strong smell of his cologne. It's worse than the "purr-fume" I wore in Hollywood!

"Brad!" exclaims Patricia. "How simply wonderful to see you again!"

"Oh *no*," Amelia whispers to me, trying to hide us both behind a tall filing cabinet. "Pie, do you remember Brad Carter?"

forget? I was *nearly* in a ...rcial that he was directing. He was horrible to work with, pompous, and mean. When I stood up to him on set, it all went SPECTACULARLY WRONG, which led to instant fame for me and huge embarrassment for Brad.

"I'm sure you've heard about my new play— it's on the first of next month," he announces loudly. "It will truly restore my position as the GREATEST director, after recent—" his eye twitches angrily— "*hiccups.*"

"Oh! That's the same night as MY show, *The Everett Emeralds*!" exclaims Patricia cheerfully.

Brad **scowls.**

"And I have just cast a *FABULOUS* cat actor," Patricia adds. "Marshmallow Pie!"

Brad looks over and sees us, recognizing me immediately. He goes bright red with anger under his fake tan.

"Oh dear, he doesn't look happy about that," says Amelia nervously.

But I soon forget about Brad, because something much, MUCH worse happens.

Patricia catches sight of Buster.

"Hang on, haven't I seen this handsome dog somewhere before?" she asks. "It's Buster, isn't it?"

I feel immediately irritated. This is MY audition, not his.

"Did you know we're looking for a dog to appear in the play too?" she asks. "We simply *must* cast Buster—what an adorable pair you will be!"

My heart sinks. This is **TERRIBLE** news.

Chapter Three
An Actor's Life for Me

The day before rehearsals begin, Amelia, Buster, and I are invited to the Theater Royale to look around and to meet everybody.

"Darlings—come in, come in!" Patricia exclaims, greeting us on the steps.

As we walk into the foyer, I see my reflection in a huge fancy gold mirror. I can't help noticing how good my fluffy white fur looks against the plush red velvet.

I know I'm going to *LOVE* the theatrical life. My only problem is Buster. I feel sure he's going to try to spoil it for me.

We are led along a steep narrow hallway and out onto the stage itself, where the other actors are waiting to meet us.

I gaze across the rows of empty seats, imagining the night of the show when the audience will be there, all looking at me adoringly.

Then Patricia calls us over. "The play takes place in Everett House," she tells us, gesturing around the grand drawing room we are standing in. "Buster, Pie, you both belong to Lord and Lady Everett."

She points out two people sitting on a luxurious sofa covered in satin pillows.

"HARRUMPH," grumbles Lord Everett, hardly looking up from his newspaper, but Lady Everett smiles and waves. I jump up next to her and make myself comfortable. This will suit me just fine.

"Another important character in the play," says Patricia, "is Miss Honeyblossom."

"I spend a lot of time sitting in this armchair, knitting," Miss Honeyblossom explains. "I may look like nothing more than a dear old lady, but I am secretly a BRILLIANT detective!"

I like Lady Everett because she is *glamorous* and *elegant* like me. I also like Miss Honeyblossom, because she rummages in the pocket of her cardigan and brings out a crunchy cat treat for me.

Then she accidentally drops her knitting, and Buster picks it up for her. Out of her other pocket she gets a dog treat for him. **INFURIATING.** He might *seem* nice, but I feel sure he's just trying to hog the attention.

The Case

STASHED IN THE ATTIC

FOUND

MISSING

Patricia tells us that after the emeralds are stolen, we have very important detective roles in helping to solve the case.

"Buster, you will sniff out the clues and find the cat burglar's mask," she says. "Pie, you will go up into the attic and discover the loot stashed there.

THE SUSPECT

THE CULPRIT

You see, it turns out the thief is posing
as a mysterious cat burglar, but is
actually the maid, living right under
their very roof . . . Don't worry, you can
still keep an eye on the action through
the gap in the attic hatch. It's a trapdoor
built into the set."

But Buster doesn't seem to be listening. There's a slight rustling noise behind the curtain at the side of the stage, and for a moment, I think I can smell cologne. With ears pricked up and nose twitching, Buster jumps up and hurries over. He sniffs around, as if someone was there.

"What's the matter, Buster?" Patricia says, frowning a little. She walks over to the curtain and peers behind it. "See— there's nobody here! It must have been the wind."

Of course, I think to myself. *Silly dog.* He's probably trying to let everyone know what a good actor he is, showing off his "detective skills", but he's just being a nuisance.

Just wait until the real acting begins. If he thinks he can outshine me, he's in for a BIG surprise!

Chapter Four
The Everett Emeralds

The next morning Amelia drops us off at the theater for the first day of rehearsals. Irritatingly, Buster hurtles on ahead, but I hurry to catch up.

"Have a great time!" says Amelia, unpacking our bowls, food, and brushes from her bag. "I'll be back to pick you up at the end of the day."

THE EVERETT
EMERALDS

COMING SOON!

As soon as the play starts,
I am determined to
attract attention with
a FANTÅSTĨC
performance.

I saunter splendidly across the stage. . . .

54

I play charmingly with a ball of wool
from Miss Honeyblossom's knitting
basket . . .

55

. . . and then I sit grandly next to Lady Everett on the sofa, sinking into the plump satin pillows. She is wearing the *Everett Emeralds*—an ornate green necklace, bracelet, and earrings. They catch the light, shimmering, and twinkling.

"They really match the green of your eyes!" Lady Everett says to me. I give her my most sparkling look.

But Buster INSISTS on trying to compete with me. He makes a big show of being distracted, looking around with an agitated expression. Then he starts sniffing at that curtain again.

A moment later he returns, carrying what looks like a silk handkerchief in his mouth. He drops it at Patricia's feet, tail wagging expectantly.

"Silly dog!" she says. "This isn't the cat burglar's mask you're meant to find— and we haven't even gotten to that part of the play yet." She casts the handkerchief aside. "Okay, everyone—let's try that scene again!"

What a show-off Buster is, with his
display of being the brilliant detective
who finds all the clues. But he didn't
even get it right!

HA.

I am certain he is trying to upstage me. I
don't trust him ONE BIT.

That evening at home, after our dinner, Amelia entertains Buster by throwing a rubber ball around the room. She laughs as he leaps through the air.

"Come on, Pie!"
she calls over to me.

"You usually love a bouncy ball.
Come and join in!"

It's true, I do. I feel a tingle in my paws
to jump up and play, but I don't give
in. I won't fall for Buster's fake charms.
Instead I sit on my own and stare fixedly
out of the window while Amelia and
Buster carry on having fun.

Chapter Five
In the Doghouse

It's the second day of rehearsals. Buster and I are waiting on the stage, while the human actors are out at lunch. Patricia told us to have a good rest, because this afternoon we have a BIG scene to work on: the cat burglar is going to sneak in and steal the *Everett Emeralds*!

Buster is dozing in his dog bed. I find an unattended vendor's tray and some salty crumbs to lick, then I settle down for a little nap too.

POPCORN! CHIPS!

All of a sudden, Buster leaps to his feet, ears pricked up. I hear it too—somebody is walking across the attic above us and rattling the trapdoor.

Buster starts barking loudly. We hear the **crash** of something being dropped, then the sound of heavy footsteps thundering down the hidden staircase and hurrying away. I just catch a glimpse of a looming figure disappearing behind the curtain.

Strange, I think, licking the last stray crumbs from my whiskers, *I didn't think the others were back yet*, but I assume that must have been the cat burglar actor, rehearsing the scene already.

WOOF! WOOF! WOOF!

Buster's barking has built up to a **frenzy,** however. He rushes across the stage, knocking over a chair, and charges up the staircase to the attic.

At this moment Patricia and the other actors return from lunch.

"What's all this commotion?" Patricia says, hearing Buster overhead. "Come down from there!"

When Buster reappears, he is beside himself, whining and whimpering, tugging at her pant leg as if urging her to follow him.

"Settle down, Buster!"

she tells him firmly. "What a ridiculous fuss about nothing! I'm not at all impressed with your behavior."

Buster slumps miserably as Patricia turns away from him.

"Take your positions, everybody," she says. "We will now start rehearsing the cat burglar scene."

That's odd, I think to myself. *Haven't some of us just been doing that?* Of course not everyone has the natural ability I have. Perhaps the cat burglar actor needs some extra practice.

The scene takes place at night, with only me and Buster on stage, pretending to be asleep. The lights are turned down low, the room lit only by the moonlight coming in through the window.

I hear the footsteps cross the attic again and continue down the hidden staircase. This time, though, they are much softer and quieter.

The secret door silently opens, and the cat burglar slips into the drawing room. I can't resist having a little peek.

The Theft of The Everett Emeralds

I watch as she opens the jewelry box on the desk, takes the *Everett Emeralds* and other precious gems . . .

retraces her steps to secretly stash the loot in the attic . . .

and then I lose sight of her as she goes
out through the skylight and away over
the rooftops.

It's strange, though. This cat burglar seems different—smaller and more light-footed. So if this is the REAL cat burglar . . .

then who was that up in the attic before?

Chapter Six
You're BUSTED, Buster!

Today is the last day of rehearsals before the performance tomorrow.

Everybody is gathered in the drawing room after the burglary has been discovered. Lady Everett is holding out her empty jewelry box.

"Gone! GONE!" she cries.

"The *Everett Emeralds* have been *stolen*!"

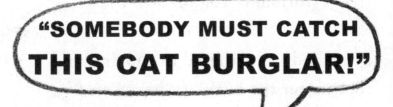

"SOMEBODY MUST CATCH THIS CAT BURGLAR!"

Lord Everett roars.

Miss Honeyblossom says nothing and carries on with her knitting, but she is looking carefully around the room.

As Patricia told us to do, Buster begins his search to sniff out the clues. I slip out through the secret door, and scurry up the staircase into the attic to discover the hidden loot.

There's lots of other stuff up here as well—a vase, an antique clock, a fancy china teapot . . .

And there's a screwdriver too, which seems a bit out of place.

I settle down. It's warm and cozy up here, and as Patricia said, I can still keep an eye on the action below through the crack in the trapdoor.

But what's this I can hear? It's Buster's heavy paws bounding up the staircase. DISASTER. I didn't close the secret door behind me and now Buster has followed me up! He bursts into the attic, charges over to me, and—the OUTRAGE—nips me on the bottom! I leap off the trapdoor with a yowl.

This is the **LAST STRAW.** I would like
to box Buster's ears, but there's no time.
Hearing the rumpus above her, Patricia
calls us both down.

yowl

"BUSTER, YOUR BEHAVIOR IS UNACCEPTABLE!"

she says. "You had a very important role in this scene, and instead you went to chase a CAT! SO unprofessional. You are putting your entire acting career at risk."

This time Buster looks frustrated, and growls.

He's in the doghouse now. Ha, that will teach him a lesson for trying to ruin everything for me.

When Amelia picks us up at the end of the rehearsal, she takes one look at us and her face falls.

"Oh *no*," she says. "You two are in a really bad mood with each other!"

On the way home, we bump into Zack, Amelia's friend from school. He is just walking back from the pet store with his kitten, my little buddy Gingernut.

"How's the play going?" he asks Amelia.
When he sees her troubled expression,
he suggests that we all go to our favorite
kiosk for a hot chocolate.

"I'm really anxious about the performance tomorrow," Amelia is saying to Zack while they sip their drinks. "Pie and Buster are getting on so badly— what if it spoils the show?"

"Don't worry," says Zack. "I'll be there to support you. Besides, Pie is pure class. He won't let anything stand in the way of being a superstar!"

Feeling more cheerful now, I sneak a nibble of whipped cream from Amelia's hot chocolate while she's not looking. A big blob goes on my nose. I don't think anyone noticed.

Yes. Pure class, that's me.

Buster's owner has returned from her work trip in time for the performance. So when we get back to our apartment, she comes up to collect Buster and all his belongings.

I am **delighted** to see him go.

Chapter Seven
Catastrophe

All day, Amelia is on tenterhooks, anxiously waiting for tonight's performance. But I'm not nervous. I am a superstar—I won't let Buster drag me down with his terrible behavior. I'm confident I will *shine*.

Amelia puts on her best dress and she, her dad, and I set out for the Theater Royale, picking up Zack on the way. The theater looks magical, all lit up at night.

They drop me off backstage with the other actors, and take their seats in the front row.

Buster's owner is here too, sitting further along. There is an expectant hush. Then the curtain goes up, and the show begins.

The play goes smoothly, and we perform our roles perfectly. Until near the end. . . .

We are all gathered for the final scene, with Lady Everett holding out her empty jewelry box.

Again, Buster is sniffing out the clues and I go up to the attic, among the stolen loot, and enjoy the view through the crack in the trapdoor.

Ha ha, Buster, I think to myself. *I shut the secret door behind me, so you won't be able to follow me this time!*

That's odd, though . . . Why is Buster frantically dragging pillows over from the sofa to the spot right underneath where I am sitting?

There's an ominous creaking from the trapdoor hinge.

"I can now reveal that the *true* identity of the cat burglar is closer to home than you think!" Miss Honeyblossom is saying below, turning to the maid. "And it is . . ."

But just at that moment, the trapdoor
swings open and I am

falling . . .

falling . . .

falling . . .

all tangled up in the stolen jewelry.

Thank goodness I land—**WHOOMPH**—
on the soft bed of pillows that Buster has
arranged.

I am followed by the screwdriver, which
falls and rolls away across the stage.

The audience gasp. They are on the edge
of their seats.

Now the teapot is toppling down from the attic too! It's coming straight toward my head . . .

but Buster leaps through the
air and catches it in his mouth just
in time.

There is a moment of absolute silence, the audience hardly daring to breathe.

Miss Honeyblossom improvises beautifully.

"As I was saying," she proclaims with a flourish, now pointing at me, "the real cat burglar is actually . . . THE CAT!"

I'm shocked by what just happened—but I know the show must go on! So I join in, smiling at the audience as if to say, "Yes, it was ME all along!"

I untangle myself from the jewelry, adjust the emerald bracelet to make a glamorous tiara, and swagger confidently to the front of the stage. I bow deeply.

The audience bursts into laughter and *wild* applause.

HOORAY!

HA HA HA

Bravo!

I would usually love nothing more than to soak up the adoration of the audience, but this time I'm distracted by other thoughts. *Why* did the trapdoor break?

I think of the screwdriver, which seemed out of place in the attic. . . . Could somebody have used it to meddle with the hinges?

I think back to the day of rehearsals when I THOUGHT the cat burglar actor was up in the attic, rattling the trapdoor . . . but it hadn't quite made sense.

I see it now. Buster was trying to tell us something! There was an intruder

here, right under our noses, and whoever it was sabotaged the trapdoor! When Buster raised the alarm, they dropped the screwdriver in their hurry to get away.

So *that's* why Buster pushed me off the trapdoor yesterday— to stop me from getting hurt, because he knew it was broken.

Right from the start, I've thought the worst of Buster. I judged him, mistrusted him, and ignored his warnings, when all along I'd been in great danger. I was wrong. Buster got into trouble and risked his whole career, just for me.

I step to one side to allow Buster to join me in the spotlight. He is greeted by huge whoops and cheers from the audience. *Quite right too*, I think to myself.

I realize something else as well. Amelia made Buster welcome in our home because she is so kind. But I missed out on the fun we could all have had together because I was determined not to like him, even though none of it was his fault.

I look over at Amelia in the front row, clapping and smiling. I'm very lucky to have such good friends.

Chapter Eight
A Great Team

As soon as the curtain comes down, Buster and I work together on one more important task—to show everybody the truth and unmask the REAL villain!

Amelia, her dad, Zack, and Buster's owner all come quickly to see us.

"I hope you're all right, Pie!" says Amelia.

"Did something happen to the set?" her dad asks Patricia.

Before Patricia can answer, I meow loudly at her, circling her legs, urging her to follow me.

I lead her to where the screwdriver has rolled.

Everyone gathers round. Patricia looks at the screwdriver, then up at the trapdoor hinge with its missing screws.

"The trapdoor was deliberately broken!" she exclaims. "But by WHO?"

Then Buster tugs at her sleeve, and we
all follow him to where he has carefully
stored the handkerchief he found behind
the curtain. He picks it up and puts it
into Patricia's hand.

"So this is what you were trying to show me that day. Someone left behind a silk handkerchief," says Patricia. Lifting it to her nose, she adds, "Hmm, it has a faint smell of men's cologne." I smell it too. It takes me back to my audition at the agency . . .

"Look!" says Amelia, examining it more closely. "It has initials embroidered on it—B.C."

We all look at each other with a dawning realization.

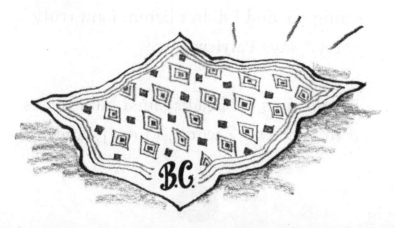

"It was **BRAD CARTER!**"
Amelia bursts out.

"What a jealous, spiteful man," Patricia
fumes. "He wanted to ruin our show—
for Pie especially."

I see it all now. On the very first day at
the theater, Buster noticed Brad lurking
behind the curtain, overhearing that I
would be on the trapdoor. Brad must have
dropped his handkerchief by mistake.

"Buster, you tried to tell me what was
going on, and I didn't listen. I am truly
sorry," says Patricia.

Buster rubs his head against her arm, as
if to say, "Don't worry, I understand."

Amelia turns to Buster's owner. "Buster was a hero!" she says.

Buster's owner smiles. "And Pie was wonderful too," she replies. "He was so brave to finish the scene even after his fall—a true performer!"

I give Buster a little nose bump. He wags his tail and gives me a slobbery lick. For once, I don't mind. Instead of being rivals, I see now that we make a great team.

And as for Brad . . .

"He must be at his own play tonight," says Patricia, "assuming that HIS show will be a success, and ours will be a disaster. But for putting my leading star in peril," she adds, glancing at me, "the police will be waiting for him."

And with a steely look, she picks up the phone.

The next morning, Amelia is giving me my breakfast.

Then she puts my new favorite show on the iPad for me, which is **MOUSE MAGIC**, while she helps her dad load the dishwasher.

A little while passes. *Have I had my breakfast?* I wonder. *No, I don't think I have.* I go into the kitchen to find that my food bowl is EMPTY. I may not survive the next hour.

Amelia's dad picks up the newspaper from the doormat.

"Look, Pie!" he says. "You're on the front page!"

Heroes!

"I'm SO proud of you, Pie—you were amazing!" says Amelia happily, giving me a hug. "And I'm so glad you weren't hurt. I've been thinking . . . Buster was really brave, wasn't he, when he saved you from the fall and the teapot? I'd like to write a piece about him in the **Fluffington Post,** if you wouldn't mind?"

I **purr** loudly to say I think that would be a great idea.

Later, I am sitting out on the balcony.
Buster is out too, on his balcony below.
It is very quiet and calm. I realize now
that all those times he used to bark and
try to jump up at me, he was just being
playful and friendly.

I notice that Buster doesn't have his black leather jacket on anymore. Instead he is wearing a lavender bow tie that Miss Honeyblossom knitted for him. He gives me a happy look as if to say, "This is much more *me*."

And I am wearing my FRUITY onesie, because what's one or two buttons coming open between friends?

I listen to the hum of the traffic in the streets below, blending together with my purring, and my eyes are closing, closing . . .

purr

I feel peaceful and safe. I'm so relieved that Brad got his comeuppance. And I know now that even a superstar like me can make room in the spotlight for others—every now and again.

The End

Check out the other books in the series...

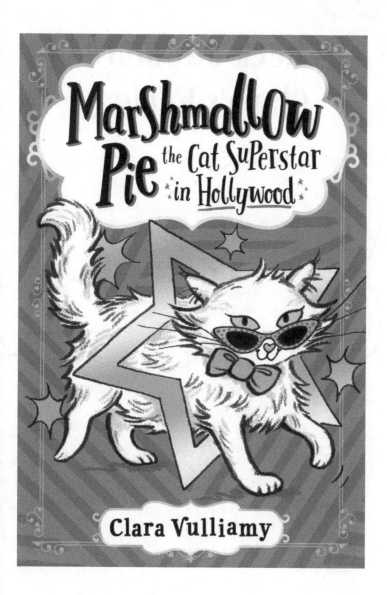

Check out more of Clara's books...